Elm

Cherry

Aspen

Mimosa

Alder

Cottonwood

Sycamore

Redbud

Laburnum

Dogwood

Hickory

Tilia Tuan

Chestnut

Birch

Pawpaw

Tamarack

Ginkgo

To books about friendship that lead to cherished friendships and
the wonderful experience of creating more books together
—B.F. and T.L.

STICK AND STONE

BEST FRIENDS FOREVER!

BETH FERRY · TOM LICHTENHELD

HOUGHTON MIFFLIN HARCOURT · BOSTON · NEW YORK

Stick.

Stone.

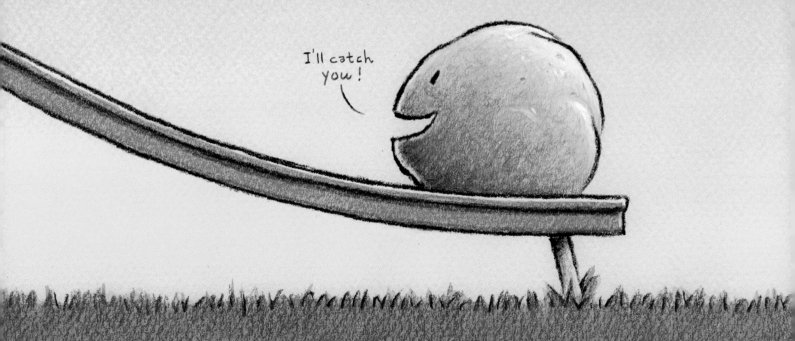

A friendship full-grown.

Together they'll venture
into the unknown.

Stick's on a search
for maple or birch.

"Am I a spruce,

a willow,

an oak?

Where did I live before
my branch broke?"

Stick is excited.
Stone?
Quite delighted.

"I love a good quest."

"Quests are the best!"

They wander,
explore

through forests galore.

Through valleys and creeks

and high mountain peaks.

But Stick doesn't see
his family tree.

"I think
it was
big.

I think
it was
tall."

Stone giggles, "Stick!
That sounds like them ALL."

The forest is vast.
The forest is deep.
Soon they are lost
in shadows that creep.

They hear something scurry.
"C'mon, Stick. Let's hurry."
"Was that a bear?"
"Was it a snake?"
"It might be a monster."
"THIS WAS A MISTAKE!"

Stone looks at Stick.
Stick looks at Stone.

They both slowly turn,
then scream, "It's . . .

"Pinecone!"

Stick.
Stone.
No longer alone.

Stick.
Stone.
Saved by Pinecone.

Now homeward bound.
Now safe and sound.

"Stick!" replies Stone.
"Your family's ME!"

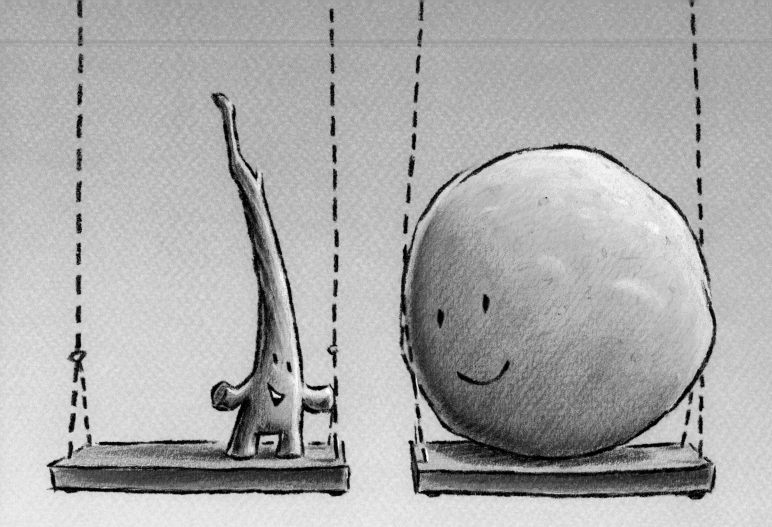

"You're right," whispers Stick.
"You're right next to me.
You always have been."

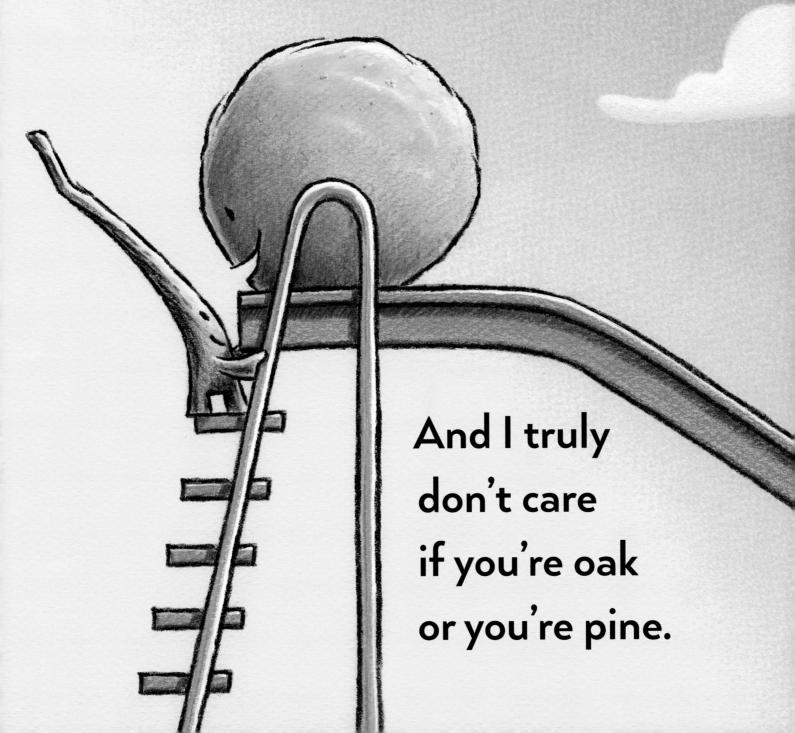

"And I always will be.

And I truly
don't care
if you're oak
or you're pine.

"I'm your best friend . . .

and you'll always be mine."

The End